Shadow Chasers

Lindsay Petersen

Published by Lindsay Peet, 2024.

This is a work of fiction. Similarities to real people, places, or events are entirely coincidental.

SHADOW CHASERS

First edition. August 30, 2024.

Copyright © 2024 Lindsay Petersen.

ISBN: 979-8227392107

Written by Lindsay Petersen.

Table of Contents

SHADOW CHASERS

I

"**H**old on, hold **on** *now – you're telling me I said what?*"

Six excited voices in five languages and pitches explained everything to him in fifteen seconds.

Nofina Nolana shook his head – carefully, gently. Multiple shots of clear liquor did not aid clear thinking the next morning, and he struggled to work his way through the six renditions of his past twenty-four hours. A rapid review of the crew arrayed along the walls of the boat's cabin, more shiny and sanitary than he was accustomed to, he chuckled. Whatever they'd done it looked like the results were good, but he still craved details. "And one more time—what did we do?'

Again the voices flooded over him, much the same but slightly different. Nolana smiled ruefully, winced and put a palm up – silence reigned. "You," he pointed at the man he considered his lieutenant, whom he called Juan, "explain to me please just where I am and why. Without going too far in the past, please. My brain can't handle first causes just now."

"*Sí.* Last night we talked about the sun's e-clipse coming soon, and you said we should steal a boat and go to Alaska to where we can see the moon hide the sun. 'Once in a lifetime opportunity' you said." He shrugged, explained, "When we found this boat with open hatches and nobody but ... *los tecnicos*" – "Engineers," offered Nolana – "*Sí,* engineers only were on board we knew that God was presenting us with a way to Alaska. We convinced *los tecnicos* to take us to Alaska. Once you explained to them what we were doing they want to see e-clipse too, and so off we go."

Nolana pondered all this. It sounded very like the kind of mischief he might do, what some might call hijinks but others hijack, the sort of exploit that would earn him drinks in saloons forlife, but the fact he had no memory of doing it troubled him. Half the fun of being Nofina Nolana, the man with 'NO FIrst NAme and NO LAst NAme', was sharing the exploits of Nofina Nolana, and if he was having blackouts his life – and the lives of his audiences – would be much diminished.

At least for this exploit others could supply details, particulars that he would later embellish as his listeners expected, even demanded. The problem was serious but not urgent, did not require drastic action just yet, but he would have to allow it to simmer on his back burner. "So you say we're heading to Alaska?"

"'Yes,'" sounded in five tongues. *So much noise!*

Softly he asked, "Whereabouts in Alaska? I hear it's a big place."

"Just as you told us. Juneau."

"Well, maybe I told you last night, but right now I *don't* know. Where?"

Juan shrugged and repeated, "Juneau."

His crew knew better than to mess with Nofina Nolana when suffering from a hangover, as he was now. Still softly, but firmly, "No, I *don't* know, and if you don't tell me now I'm going to start punching somebody."

Juan looked confused. "*Jefe*, we go to Juneau Alaska to see the e-clipse in five days."

"There's a place in Alaska called 'Juneau'?" All nodded. "Who knew?"

"Last night, you knew. Juneau. *Jefe.*"

Huh. This oyster pirate life was wearing him out. Maybe he should investigate another, less fraught lifestyle. But the scuffles, the escapes, the booty, the camaraderie, the respect of his fellow freebooters – how empty life would seem without all that! 'Yo ho yo ho the pirate's life for me' he hummed. "So we left San Francisco what, ten hours ago?"

"Twelve. *Jefe.*"

"Right, okay, half a day then. How far up the coast are we?"

"*Jefe*, this boat, she is very fast, and she travels under the water."

"And she's *supposed* to do that? The underwater thing?"

"*Si. Los tecnicos* tell me she is called 'The Nautilus' and she is famous. Already we are past Coos Bay."

Hmmm, impressive. "But this Nautilus, she's famous you say? Are we in trouble for stealing her? I mean, more trouble than usual?"

Tunku pushed his way in front. "She is famous as boat of disappeared underwater pirate! Cannot complain!"

So much to digest. "To be clear, then, we're in a stolen underwater pirate ship sailing to Juneau Alaska to see a once-in-a-lifetime e-clipse."

Another wave of happy agreement. "Well, all right then. Good not to be in the dark, but I guess that's part of the whole e-clipse shadow hunting adventure."

VICTORIA BEARSKIN FRETTED over her hair. "'Beautiful blue-black tresses'! Pfui!" she muttered, mocking her characterless hair. "But can I *do* anything with them? NO! Like some serpent it wriggles free of any clips or ribbons, and in no time I look like some Plains savage!" In frustration she tore its restraints free and watched it tumble sleekly about her shoulders in the mirror. Her fingers combed it away from her face in loving frustration – it *did* have a lovely luster and body, and framed her exasperated expression kindly.

The finest dress she possessed was a simple day dress, but it was clean, unpatched, and not-so-far out of style, so would have to do for her request of the head of Vassar's scientific department. Mavis Mitchell already had organized the astronomical expedition of young women 'umbraphiles' travelling to Denver, and Victoria was determined to be added in.

It troubled her that she hadn't even been invited. Surely her observatory work was worthy, and her character was unblemished. Professor Mitchell had fought long and hard for the women's right to vote; surely she could not object to a spirited advocacy by one of her pupils, especially a tribal woman.

"Good morning, Miss Bearskin. A pleasure to see you. How may I help you this day?" Ms. Mitchell asked. Was she already wary?

A deep breath, then, "Professor Mitchell, I believe I could prove a valuable member of the party travelling to Denver for the eclipse. You are aware, I'm sure, of my observations of asteroids, and of the moonlets orbiting Jupiter and Saturn. I would bring these same observational skills to this once-in-a-lifetime heavenly event, and boost further Vassar's growing reputation in the world of science." There, she sighed—she'd gotten it out, almost as she'd imagined it, logically and persuasively, in the calm voice of science and reason.

Ms. Mitchell took her time, weighing her words. "Miss Bearskin, it is true that your work has been exemplary, and your reputation beyond question. There is the issue, however, of your ... background. Your tribe – the Wyandottes, I believe?" Victoria nodded, her heart sinking – "was among those fighting for slavery in our nation's recent struggles."

"But –"

Ms. Mitchell waved away her objections. "Moreover, the directors share a concern for your own safety. To this day we hear tales of native resistance leading to bloodshed. It was only two years ago that General Custer and his men were massacred! And not far from our destination! It is the shared opinion of the directors that sending a single Wyandotte woman into the Territories would imperil her safety."

"But," she paused in case Ms. Mitchell wasn't yet done destroying her dream, "Denver is not a Territory any more. It became a state in August, two years ago. It's civilized."

The flat gaze of Ms. Mitchell told Victoria that the date Colorado became a state was immaterial. "Civilization does not occur overnight, neither to a territory nor to a people. It is still the Wild West, and I can't send Victoria Bearskin of the Wyandotte tribe to a lawless land of wild prospectors and wilder ... *natives*."

"I see," Victoria bowed her head, acknowledging the hopelessness of overcoming the prejudices masked by reason and compassion. "I thank you for your time." She turned to leave.

"Miss Bearskin, I hope this does not discourage you in your studies. You do show great promise."

Manners mandated a 'thank you,' but Victoria's throat choked on the words as she hurried away from her interview with America's most prominent woman scientist.

After a good cry in her room she slowly undressed, thinking to change into a more comfortable everyday dress and shoes, but as she opened the drawer she noticed her old buckskin trousers, the ones she had crafted and worn in Missouri. They would still fit—seized by her dream she removed her chemise, pulled on a muslin one-piece shortall, then the trousers, and finally one of her old linen workshirts. In the mirror she admired the purposeful look of her ensemble. With a flat cap and boots she could go anywhere out west like so many leaving behind the manners and classes of the East.

In fact, she would not go to the safety of Denver, but rather she would dare to observe the once-in-a-lifetimes astronomical event from the Wyoming Territory – and who knew, she might even vote for the President! *Put that in your stupid peace-pipe and smoke it, Professor Mavis Mitchell– and I hope you cough!*

During her time at Vassar Victoria managed to set aside an emergency fund, dimes and dollars earned or sent by her tribe in support of their eastern college prodigy. Yes, she would ride the locomotive west and establish her credentials in the world, earn a reputation, bring pride to the Wyandottes!

But what sort of reputation? Attractive young Indian women with lustrous locks were common enough in the West. She would need serious equipment to prove her bona fides to doubters – she wouldn't be a beggar, earning only pity or scorn for her dreams. She had an idea, an adventurous idea, and a devilish smile curved her lips as she slipped her bustier into her carpet bag. Quickly she reviewed the contents of her gladstone bag, its curative powders and potions derived from her grandmother's teachings.

A quick look around her room, hastily tossed coat and cap, extra underclothes and shirts and brushes and soaps stuffed into her bag – she laughed, excepting the lack of dust it now looked like her room had lain vacant for months! – she pulled on her boots, donned a broad-brimmed man's hat, and shut the door on her days at Vassar.

A BEMUSED HANK LURIE watched the bewildered Englishman look this way and that, then the other way and another besides, even a quick glance up at the nearby belfry. Clearly he'd lost somebody, and if he wasn't yet he would soon be desperate for a guide – for Hank Lurie's guidance, in fact.

"Good day, sir, you appear to be somewhat adrift. Might you accept my assistance?"

It seemed the gent was not expecting help to materialize not a yard away and was momentarily flummoxed. "What? What's that? Hmm, yes, thank you, perhaps you might be of assistance." More rapid searches, this way and that. "You ... you haven't seen my manservant about, have you?"

"Perhaps. What does he look like?"

"Oh, you know, typical manservant type, correct upright posture, supercilious sneer on his lips, everything about him *just so*."

"Hmm, no, but I'll keep my eye out for him. Fella like that ought to stand out in this crowd. Until he shows up, anything I might guide you through – or to?"

The gent continued swivelling his head. "Hmm, well, yes, I suppose so. The boat won't wait forever, and my trunk is already on board. Where might I find the Missouri Queen?"

Lurie smiled ingratiatingly. "I see, heading out west then. Planning to enjoy the once-in-a-lifetime experience of the total solar eclipse?" he raised his eyebrows as if he didn't already know. "The pursuit of science in the modern age, with steam and aetherwaves showing the way."

The gent nodded uneasily, smiled weakly. Pleased that he'd read the gent aright and his investment in the manservant's distraction was not wasted, Lurie's pleasure was genuine. "I'll be happy to accompany you to the Queen, sir. It's not far, but the way can be … fraught." He put his hand out. "My name is Lurie, Hank Lurie. Follow me and we'll be at her wharf soon enough."

"Yes, but I wonder, oughtn't I continue to look for my manservant?"

Lurie pulled his hand back to check his pocket watch. "Yes, you may, but you haven't much time, and for all we know he coulda been shanghaied, tied up in the hold of an outbound freighter. Or sleeping off a bender in a flophouse or bordello. New Orleans is a city with many perils and pleasures," he raised a knowing eyebrow.

The gent looked Hank up and down. "Yes, I see, I well believe you might be acquainted with both the perils and pleasures of this town." After that backhanded compliment – or underhanded insult – the gent put out his hand. "Jonathan Clark of Kent. Pleasure to make your felicitous acquaintance, Mr. Lurie. Well then, as the Frenchies say, '*on y va*'. I believe I heard some mongrel variant of that tongue here."

"I've heard tell they say things a bit different here, to be sure," and he led the way. Clark delayed enough for one more reconnaissance of the plaza then turned to follow. Lurie breathed deep in relief – there was no knowing how long the manservant would be distracted by Mme. Coucher's charms, and it would spoil the schemer's plans if the upright and proper manservant were to trot out of her establishment buttoning up his drawers and hollering just then.

Only after Mr. Clark was properly settled into his grand cabin did Lurie look to his own lodgings aboard. He wouldn't feel completely safe from the manservant's intercession until the final ropes were cast off, but he did grant himself a healthy swig from his hip flask. Things were coming together nicely.

In the main parlor he set about penciling his despatch for the Post, and a second for the Herald under one of his many pen names. The eclipse stoked so much excitement in readers hungry for the exploits of adventurers and the thrilling world of science that his work for the Post and Herald would earn him a pretty penny or two, get him the reputation he deserved.

His drafts done he ordered a rye whiskey stretched out his legs he chuckled. He would demand reimbursement for expenses twice on this two-month trip, and those expenses would add up rapidly. The Englishman appeared to be the type who was eager for adventures of the right sort and necessarily dependent on his guide – a role Lurie was happily filling, and for which he hoped to be paid handsomely by a man who likely gambled guineas on the flip of a card or the nose of a thoroughbred. Rose-colored glasses were too prosaic for the journey Lurie anticipated. Although it was a 'once-in-a-lifetime' experience, he fervently hoped it wouldn't turn out to be the highlight of his journalistic career.

II

Any fool could see this 'Nautilus' was a sleek craft. The interior lacked the cracks and crevices every other ship his crew had shared – there was neither dust nor smudges on the gleaming metal walls he saw during a quick tour. As they were still underwater Nolana had only the vaguest idea of what her skin looked like, if it matched the inside's ultra-modern sheen or if it surpassed what he'd run his fingertips over. His only chance to get a clue of the Nautilus' shape had come when staggering aboard. It had been a foggy night and he'd been blind drunk, leastways that was what he told himself. And now going on deck was impossible until *los tecnicos* opted to raise her above the ocean's surface. He had no idea what kept her down or might allow her to float, but he supposed that sooner or later she'd come up and he could get a handle on what was what.

Lieutenant Juan had ordered the boat's engineers to keep her submerged; his *jefe* could only guess why that was but he saw no cause to countermand the order, so under the waves they hummed northwestward. The only outside distraction from the smooth-running tranquillity inside was at the bow, where panoramic glass revealed all the undersea life that ocean swimmers preferred not to think about. Teeth and fins rushed past willy-nilly as the submarine's prow barged through the ichthyan predators and schools, endlessly repeated dramas of hungry pursuit and momentary escape.

Nolana idly repaired a split seam on his waistband as the thrillers raced past. An odd question drifted into his skull—where can a fish go to hide? A fish must swim to breathe, and wherever it swam it was immersed in water, stuff that was clear as … water. Speed and trickery could delay the end, but speed slacked as one aged, and trickery's deceptions had to be perfect – every time.

With his own eyes he'd witnessed the 'flying fish' of Santa Catalina Island, leaping from the waves and soaring for dozens of feet, disappearing from the vision of the drooling dolphins chasing them below the surface. How might *he* flee to another dimension, leave behind no scent, no tell-tales, no tracks for the hunters or the law.

What if a fish flew so far that it came down in a different sea, one where dolphins and barracudas knew nothing about such tricks and so were fooled over and over by this clever trick? Would the fish be lonely? Some fish, he supposed, just naturally were loners. Daring fish might strike out from their schools because they realized swimming fin-to-fin with other tasty seafood snacks might feel safe, but was it truly wise?

He shook his head at such idle musings and tugged on his trousers, ensured his shirt draped over his new handiwork. He stretched this way and that and the stitches held and the fit was comfortable, even with the extra gold double eagles. Those would help him fly away when that time came.

He moseyed to the bridge, greeted Juan and asked for an update on their progress. "This boat, she is amazing, *Jefe*! So smooth, so fast – we'll be there early, plenty of time to check out the gold, the women, the mooses!"

"You and your mooses, Juan," he shook his head.

"*Jefe*, the mooses, they are gigantic!" He raised his free hand up as high as he could, then rested his side against the wheel to spread both hands, his eyes wide, his eyebrows threatening to join his hairline. "And mean!"

"Well, I hope you get to see your mooses, and some gold, and maybe a lady or two. Keep an eye out for icebergs, too – I hear that's where they come from, like it's a factory or something up there."

Juan nodded.

"I got to wondering, Juan, just why are we under the water? Are we hiding?"

"Big storm above. I look through spy tube, see big waves! See big wave come at you, wash over, I felt like I was drowning for a second! I look now, see if storm is gone." A gleaming bronze tube telescoped from the ceiling; when it stopped a pair of handles flopped out. Juan parked his hands there and looked through two eyeholes, then stepped sideways to pivot the tube. "Es bueno," he murmured. "You see, *Jefe*?" he gestured to the tube.

"What's this, Juan? Some kinda technological magic?"

"I no think so, just mirrors only."

Nolana arranged his hands and eyes on the tube and looked out at the calm north Pacific under lead skies. That could be a problem for e-clipse viewing if it held. "Well, looks like you might as well take her up, let's see how she does sailing like a normal ship."

"*Si, Jefe.*"

Nolana watched as Juan spun some valve wheels, flicked some switches and pulled some levers. Pumps hummed below and as the pitch of Nemo's amazing craft shifted back Nolana leaned forward, into the bow, toward Juneau. Maybe now he could see what this undersea marvel looked like.

VICTORIA WAS SURPRISED, then shocked, then dismayed when she saw the train she was taking west had a turret mounted on the caboose, a Gatling Gun's muzzles pointing skyward – for now. She halted, tilted her head and wondered what to make of this teasing of troubles.

Speaking of troubles – the official Vassar Solar Eclipse Scientific Expedition came up behind, chattering and giggling. It went silent when they saw Victoria. "Hey, Bearskin, what are you doing here? You didn't talk Ms. Mitchell into letting you come, did you?"

"Maybe she threatened Ms. Mitchell. Tomahawk or such."

Her posture erect, Victoria answered, "No, I'm going – but not with you."

"Well then, what are you getting at?"

Victoria thought her seven words had explained all, and didn't want to ruin their impact by repeating them. "I *am* going west, but *not* with you."

They took in her very practical travelling outfit, her buckskin trousers, man's linen shirt under her bustier, contrasting starkly to their ankle-length dresses and gloves. "Are the rest of your things already aboard?" one asked, looking at her bulging carpet bag and gladstone.

"No. This," she nodded to her things, "is all I'm taking. I intend, in my way, to live off the land," she said, unclear herself on what all that would entail.

"Indian style, then. So you are going west? You already have your ticket?"

She dropped her gladstone, reached in her reticule and held up the pasteboard. "*C'est un fait accompli,*" she said in her best Vassar French.

"A 'done deal' you say? We'll see about that," and three girls pranced off. "Good luck, Victoria," murmured the fourth – was her name Emily?—and hurried off.

Victoria laughed as she realized that, once she stepped aboard the train, all connections with her past were severed. She would taste freedom for the first time since she was a little girl – funny, little girls look forward to being able to do anything they want when they grow up, but somehow it doesn't work out that way.

Now she could be, do, and dress as anybody she wanted to. Once she put her backside on the Pullman seat her journey toward her open-ended future was firmly and irrevocably begun. No tethering friendships, no suffocating job, no burdensome home bound her to the mundane life of Victoria Bearskin. No more would she force a smile at all the tiresome jokes about her family name, holding down her anger at the mocking of the essence that name gave her. In the frontier of 'civilization' she could adopt a new name, a new self, become a self-made woman.

The words '*fait accompli*' resonated in her core; her old life was done, a new virgin life awaited her, and she assured herself there was no going back. She would take on that motto, never backing down, accepting what was done without regrets and moving ahead. 'Faye D'Accompli' would be Victoria Bearskin's new soubriquet. She laughed – she could even be Rousseau's Noble Savage if she wanted! But truer to herself than some deluded European's fantasy—Faye would not be held down by the fears of others, the doubts of others, the histories of others or their conventions.

A deep-seated angst assaulted her and her confidence flipped to a sort of sudden-onset cosmic terror, left her sweaty and shaking. The out-of-character outburst of exuberance had felt so foreign, so unnerved her that she hyperventilated while her eyes looked around desperately – but for what? What could relieve her of this nameless dread?

Oh, dear Lord, what had she done? What was she doing, what had she been thinking? Who would back her up, take her in and feed her if everything went wrong – and 'wrong' is *exactly* how everything would go, she just knew it. Her head and shoulders drooped in misery and eventually she curled up and slept. As the train began its journey to the frontiers Faye D'Accompli snored quietly in a corner.

MR. CLARK STOOD AT the Queen's bow, his ample forearms on the rail, trying to digest the vastness of the Great River and the valley he was sailing up. "Floating on the breast of the Mighty Waters, eh, Lurie?" he remarked to his companion.

"That we are, Mr. Clark, that we are. Quite a vista, don't you agree?"

"Yes, yes, that's not the only sense gratified. Not long ago I believed I smelled home cooking, but an old hand assured me 'twas only the river, 'twas only the river."

Lurie inhaled deeply, curious about what his companion might have sniffed that hinted at something edible but finally shook his head, mystified. *Perhaps it's true what they say about English cooking,* he told himself. "Soon we'll be coming into St. Louis, and there we'll be heading on up the Missouri River. That's when our journey west will truly commence."

"Ah, looking forward to it, to experiencing the Great Adventure of the American Frontier."

Lurie wondered how and why Clark managed to capitalize terms in his speech – perhaps that, too, was an English trait. "I guarantee you will get plenty of the frontier, and adventure. We're taking the 'Mighty Missouri,'" Lurie tried the capitalization thing himself but decided it didn't suit, "all the way to the Fort Union Trading Post up in the Montana Territory. There we'll turn south on the Yellowstone River and continue on westward, ever westward, high up the flanks of the Rocky Mountains. There we'll have the clearest skies for the eclipse."

Mr. Clark nodded sagely. "And you're certain we'll arrive to … those flanks in time? Wouldn't want to go all this way and then miss the damned thing, eh? The fellows at the club would mock me endlessly. 'Can't find the shadow Clark' they'd label me, or some such epithet. 'The man without a shadow'. Whatever they worked up, it's a certainty it would not be flattering."

"We've got plenty of time, Mr. Clark, plenty of time for adventure and exploration."

Clark pulled back from the rail and looked squarely at Lurie. "I say, you don't suppose there will be Indians, do you? I mean to say, Indian attacks? Scalps and whatnot?"

"Well, there are the Bannacks."

"Bannocks, you say? Oat-cake wars?"

Lurie dredged his memory – ah, yes! "I see, the Scottish oat cakes are called 'bannocks,' aren't they? If overcooked are they the victims of 'bannock burn'?"

"'Bannockburn'" he said flatly. "Do you know 'Clark' is a Scots name? My forebears hailed from Paisley. Perhaps Americans are unaware of the meaning of Bannockburn, and what it means. Robert the Bruce sent Eddie the Second off, tail 'twixt his legs. Unsure what oat cakes had to do with that." He allowed the lesson to sink in. "I take it these marauding Indians are called Bannocks?"

A properly chastened Lurie answered. "Bannacks, spelled differently. Farther west than we'll be journeying some have left the reservation and some have fought, some have killed and some have died. And of course it was only two years ago that Lieutenant Colonel Custer and his troops were slaughtered, not far from our route."

"Two years, you say? Not far, you say?"

"Not to worry, those Indians have been thoroughly and completely pacified since then. The Nez Perce ended their wanderings also. No, I don't think the Indians are a danger anymore– leastways, not compared to the grizzly bears and wolves."

"Ah, thank you, good to know, I'm truly gratified for your reminding me of the abundance of ways for me to meet my end."

"Aw, heck, you didn't expect to live forever, did ya?"

Mr. Clark turned back forward, facing the prospect of an ignominious end to his adventure, passing through the digestive tract of a fierce carnivore. He was quiet for some time, listening to the bow waves curl away into brown waters. "And," he gulped, "what of the buffalo? Do they present a danger?"

"There are just a few left, nothing like the seas of buffalo that covered the plains not so long ago. "

"A sea of buffalo. I should have liked to have seen that."

"Well, the West is changing, being tamed, and some things just don't fit in with the way things are going to be from here on out."

Conversation paused then until Lurie pointed ahead, to port. "That there's St. Louis up there. If you look down at the waters you can see how the Missouri's muddy waters aren't mixed in the Mississippi's yet," he pointed down to the two-tone waves.

"Mmm, I see."

"Out that way," Lurie swept his left arm out, "the plains roll all the way to the foothills of the Rockies. Maybe the richest farmland in all the world, and some of that soil is getting churned up by our boat as we head to the Rockies. But we can't take the Queen all the way; her draft is too deep, and there are lots of snags, broken trees in the river that'll poke holes in her. For today, though, we're docking in Saint Louie to pick up more coal, might even spend the night there. I hear tell the Big Muddy is not a river to test in the dark. 'Course, the days *are* long this time of year."

"It's heartening to hear your recklessness is not unbounded."

III

"I see no mooses at all," lamented Juan.

"Mooses? Hell, we can't even see the shore. Can't miss the waves on the rocks, though. You sure we're not going to run into anything in this pea soup?"

"No sir, we are not moving. If we did hit a thing the engineers say the boat, she is made from a miracle steel Captain Nemo invented called nemol. Very hard, doesn't rust." They looked down at the nickel-colored hull below their feet. "No rusting, no corroding, but they say it eats bronze."

"'Nemol, huh? Sounds like a patent medicine. Well, we all gotta eat something." He looked up from the hull, toward the fog-obscured shore, toward whatever islands may have been lurking unseen, then up to imagined peaks. "Juan, you got us here plenty quick, and I thank you for that. And we still have about a week until that e-clipse happens, but if this goes on I don't see how we'll ever see much of anything 'ceptin' the shortest foggy night ever!" He looked to the side, wanted to spit for emphasis but he'd quit chewing tobacco. "Any ideas?"

"This boat, she has observation balloon on a leash. Maybe you can see where fog isn't and Juan goes there."

Balloon? How would they get the hot air to lift it? "One of them hot air balloons?"

"No, *Jefe*, this one has lifting gas. In steel bottles."

"Huh. And a leash, too? Is that made out of that nemol, too?"

Juan grinned. "*Si, Jefe*, braided like rope, no rot, no rust."

Sounded safe. "Let's take 'er out, see what she looks like. Maybe I'll find you some mooses from up above."

Juan disappeared and after a couple minutes a hatch aft of the tower opened up and Juan's head poked up above deck. After wrestling with a few tangles he started pulling free a mess of white rubberized silk and nemol cords. Nolana scrambled down the ladder to the deck, looked in the hold and saw the wicker basket, some steel cylinders marked 'H2' alongside. "Wonder what that means," Nolana mused.

"This lifting gas goes two times as high as hot air," suggested Juan.

"'Twice as good,' eh? Like another patent medicine boast? You might be right at that." He looked at the underside of the hatch where step-by-step directions laid out the procedures for launching the balloon. "Might have to do with water, too – I recall something about H2O being water. Maybe this is how they make water at sea."

"Maybe. You're the smart one, *Jefe*."

Nolana nodded acknowledgment. "Looks easy enough to launch. Have you read these directions, Juan?"

"*Si*. Take maybe an hour to float."

"How high will it go, d'you suppose?"

Juan grinned. "To the moon, or the sun. Maybe you see e-clipse up close, *Jefe!*"

Nolana peered deeper inside the bay, saw the sizable spool of fine nickel-colored cord. "Nemol wire's strong, you say?"

Juan shrugged. "*Yo no sabe, Jefe*. Engineers say Nemo was genius, make strong boat – wire is strong too," like some kind of syllogism. There was some sense to his reasoning, though.

Nolana knelt on the deck, looked at this and that, touched levers and valves. "Once we go up, how do we put that H2 back in the bottles again?"

"I no think we can."

"I no think we can either. I wonder how many times we can go up with those bottles."

"I wonder too."

Hmmm.

"Okay, then, just one bottle the first time, no more. Let's take 'er out and I'll go up a ways, not too far, to where you'll still be able to see me and me you. I'll look around for mooses and clear spots, and then you crank me down. Sound good?"

Juan shrugged. "Mooses sound good. Let's do this thing."

After a couple curses and false starts the balloon took shape, a soft-sided bulb held back by a web of nemol cordage, the basket secured to the deck for the moment with braided nemol rope, loops over hooks in the bay and on the basket. Once the balloon was upright, shifting in the sea breeze and the basket tugged on the ropes Nolana and Juan shared a look and shrugged. Juan turned off the gas, disconnected the hose, then Nolana gracelessly clambered into the basket. Immediately it plopped back to the deck, the balloonists' feet poking up.

"Is that wire secured to the basket?" Nolana asked for a tenth confirmation once he was vertical.

Amused, annoyed and excited, Juan answered, "*Si, Jefe*, you are good to go when I release the hooks."

With those words the basket drifted from the deck again, Nolana nodded and Juan wrestled the ropes from the basket's hooks and the basket lurched into the heavens. The wire sang as it unspooled, the bail shuttling back and forth feeding out smoothly.

Juan saw none of this as his eyes were to the sky, to the balloon vanishing into the murk. Then, suddenly, it flared up as sunlight hit it and it glowed like an airborne egg. Hoots and hollers came from above, like some manic god was flying and rejoicing in his wings. "Mooses?" yelled Juan.

"Ha ha, mooses indeed, my friend, mooses indeed!" came the faint answer as Juan saw an arm sweep the horizon above. This was all good. The boss would guide them to where the fog wasn't and the e-clipse would enthrall the crew on the twenty-ninth – a once-in-a-lifetime experience! With mooses!

VICTORIA BOLTED AWAKE at the sound of screams. No, wait, she was Faye now, a different name for a different person. Faye D'Accompli wondered who screamed, and why?

As she replayed it to her conscious mind she thought she detected a woman's pain and fear. When a second scream tore past the soothing clickety-clack rhythm she felt the pain and fear in her own spine. She heard the conductor's rapid steps – he was two steps past her when he halted, pivoted. "Pardon me, miss—is that your bag?" he pointed to her gladstone, the bag of a doctor.

"Yes. I can help that woman. What happened?"

"Difficult birth. Can you really help her? I mean – she sounds like she might not make it."

"I'll do what I can. Start boiling water and get me some whiskey."

He looked at her uneasily.

Her slow boil went rapid. "Set your mind at ease. You're not going to have an Indian ... 'squaw' ... rampaging in an alcoholic spree. I want to sanitize my hands."

Embarrassed only a little he nodded grimly and turned back the way he came. "She's down here. Follow me. Please." As they hurried down the passageway he looked back at her. "You're a doctor, Miss?"

"I've trained as a physician, but have no certificate. Because I'm a woman."

"Well, for her sake I hope the certificate don't matter. Hell, I bet in Wyoming they won't let bein' a woman hold you back."

"I'm liking the sound of Wyoming more all the time."

By then they'd arrived at the patient. Somebody had draped a sheet over her knees to save her dignity, but the sweat, water and blood reduced her to her most fleshly maladies. Faye looked up at the conductor, barked, "Hot water, towels, whiskey," which snapped him out of loitering, then purred, "Hello, I'm Faye, what's your name?"

The woman shrieked. "No, not one of the fae, ye canna take my child for a changeling! No!"

The strange superstitions of immigrants! She wondered. She'd heard something of the legends behind the mother's fears was clueless how best to ease them. In her most soothing tones she said, "No, ma'am, my name is Faye. I'm a native healer. Please tell me your name, dear, and how long this has been going on?" She looked up hoping to see the conductor hustling back but it was too soon.

"Me name's Mary, I'm off to jine me husband Brian in the army fort. And this started nine months ago, but only started to kill me AAAAAAAAAAAAHHH!"

Thank God the conductor was coming with towels and a brown bottle. Faye took them, tucked the towels in, poured the liquor on her hands, thought a bit – Mary's was an Irish accent, wasn't it? "Mary, care for a drop?" she held the bottle. Mary nodded and Faye poured a couple of fingers into her mouth, made sure her coughs weren't from choking, then set to work. A sudden inspiration paused her; from her bag she took calming powdered chamomile and poured a few grains into the whiskey – this job would be difficult enough without Mary thrashing about. And it wasn't good whiskey anyway.

It didn't take long for Faye to determine the baby was backwards. On the reservation she'd seen careful and forceful manipulation rotate fetuses and allow the babe to start life head-first. Between the mother's screams Faye gradually brought the child about, then had a celebratory shot of whiskey – hmm, the chamomile actually made it taste better!

Her linen blouse was soaked with perspiration, her brow dripping into her eyes, but she felt ready now to guide a new spirit into the world. "Maybe we can move her to a private cabin now? Get her off the floor?"

"Well, she ain't paid for a cabin, I don't think I'm allowed to upgrade her. Lemme think, where can I put her?"

"She can have my cabin," said a woman's voice. Emily's voice. "Here's my ticket. I'll remove my things." She looked at Faye. "Shall I help carry her?"

The men looked uncomfortable. Surely carrying a woman was the duty of a gentleman, or any man – but a strange woman in Mary's condition was off-limits. Emily received a few grateful smiles for resolving the quandary. "Yes, let's," answered Faye, slowly standing and straightening her lower back. Then she squatted, gestured to Emily to mirror her, and they carried poor Mary to Emily's bed. Another woman passenger hurried behind with the towels, hot water, and whiskey.

"Thank you, Emily," Faye gasped out as the two rested on the edge of the bedframe.

"Need any help?" Emily asked.

"We'll find out."

Emily smiled at her. "Good thing you dressed for this kind of work. Imagine trying this in a dress like this, and shoes like these," she gestured to her own dress and slippers.

"Yes, a woman never knows what challenges will confront her. It's best to be prepared."

Mary screamed again and Faye bent back to work.

THEIR VOYAGE UP THE Big Muddy went well enough, probably because of the cautious nature of the captain. "Turns out all the warnings about drowned snags punching holes in hulls aren't just stories," explained Lurie as the Queen eased past another wreck.

"Do you suppose anybody died?" Clark asked.

"No way of knowing. You see that wreck here now, in these waters, and it looks like a person could wade to the shore, maybe even float their trunk across. But this disaster might have befallen during a storm, with flood waters churning every which way, bearing folks down under the foam or down over the rocks or even to get caught on a snag their own selves."

Clark shuddered and stared forward.

At the Fort Union Trading Post they switched boats to a smaller paddle boat to take them southwest, up the Yellowstone. As their possessions were transferred Clark noticed a long slender parcel in Lurie's gear. "I say, dear fellow, is that what I think it is?"

"Depends on what you think it is. It *might* be a telescope for observing the heavens."

"I suppose it might. But I somehow doubt that is what it is. Because at first blush it looked like—"

"—It looked like exactly what it is. A forty-four-caliber lever-action Henry carbine."

Lurie figured Clark would be uneasy at this, but he was surprised to see excitement on the Brit's face. "I say, are we going big game hunting? You told me about all the threats, and the buffalo, but ..." he trailed off.

"This isn't a safari – we're only hunting for the biggest shadow on the earth. But it's not wise, not prudent, to travel these new lands without protection."

Clark cleared his throat, disappointed. "I see. And where are we going next? What site have you selected for eclipse viewing? The Shadowlands?"

"I suppose you might call it that. Our route is up the Yellowstone River, which forks off just downstream of where we are," he pointed over his shoulder with a thumb, "almost all the way to Yellowstone Lake. At the waterfalls we'll get some pack animals and zig-zag through a pass to a place called Jackson Hole, right by the Tetons."

Clark tittered at that. "The Tetons, you say? Is that the name of some Indian tribe?" he snickered.

"What's so funny?"

"Ah. Of course you don't speak French. 'Tetons' means 'tits' in English. Is there a tribe called the Tits? And are we venturing into their tribal lands, lands no doubt flowing with milk and honey?"

Clark was being silly, Lurie knew, but he welcomed it. "Now that would be a picture, wouldn't it? Just think what the squaws would look like!" he laughed. "No, the Tetons are mountain peaks. Magnificent, but not as shapely as a breast, nor as welcoming."

"*C'est dommage*! How unfortunate. Well, a man can dream."

"And a man will. Our dream is down that river," he gestured upstream to the Yellowstone's confluence, "and then to the most beautiful valley you'll ever see."

"And this beautiful valley is where you might need that carbine?"

"I might. We'll be sharing the valley with others – maybe moose, elk, bear. Better to have it and not need it than need it and not have it."

"I agree, but still ...."

"We'll be just fine, don't you worry. Let me take care of a few things at the office yonder first, and then we'll be on our way."

"Lacking *tides*, I suppose *time* can await your convenience."

"Pretty much. I'll be right back. Maybe wait for me in that hotel's lounge."

"Yes, I'll do that. The sun here is harsh, fit only for mad dogs – and Englishmen. But not this Scots/Englishman, not now," he said as he wandered off to the hotel's shade, and Lurie hurried to post more aethereal updates to readers hungry for his exploits.

Interest in the "Clark/Lurie Expedition" had engulfed the nation, its unique combination of travelogue, science explainer and adventure tale dominating opinion columns, and even launching some copycat 'tribute' tales. One breathless commentator compared Clark to Jules Verne's legendary Phileas Fogg, racing across the trackless American continent to observe and analyze the United States, and finally report on the brief dance of our two celestial bodies.

Had Lurie known he was being compared to Fogg's valet Passepartout he might have objected, but as it was his editors did their best to keep him ignorant of the sensation his reports were causing under both names. It soon became obvious to those in the trade that the scribblers Hank Lurie and Lawrence Hughes were the same scribbler, but nobody quibbled over scribblers double-dipping. In fact, knowledgeable Americans took secret pleasure at a distant newspaperman putting one over on the publishers.

Lacking any true images of the pair artists had free rein to contrive whatever likenesses they could. Across the globe boys and young men woolgathered, imagining accompanying the pair in their various guises, and young ladies dreamily contrived a lover from the conflicting fragments in print.

When Lurie learned of their efforts he surmised his publishers were wary of demands for more money had he learned of the revenue coming in for the two papers. After flurries of angry aethergrams were ignored, when he at last stormed into the offices of the two rags he was still livid, threatening legal action and hinting at more underhanded justice.

The rapid release of his book detailing – and embellishing – his adventures made him so wealthy he decided not to prosecute the penny-pinching ways of his bosses, providing they each praised his book every week for a year. By that time he was well into writing its sequel.

IV

Cautiously they repositioned the Nautilus to a spot that promised to have less fog – but would it be fog-free on the big day at the right time? One the twenty-ninth would they be able to watch the eclipse? It was a gamble, as they would not know until that day if their roll of the dice would come up craps.

Nofina Nolana was touched by the faith of his crew that he would deliver them to the ideal spot. He felt on the hook, too, as this whole voyage had been his idea, launched during a drunken binge in San Francisco Bay when an abandoned broadsheet blew against his ankles – in the fog, he now recalled.

He went pensive. Since the war he'd felt in a fog of one sort or another. Slave-owning Creole society had collapsed once the Yankees took the river, and Nofina had suddenly found himself ill-suited for the hardscrabble world of the defeated. Exquisite manners, a fine education and the arrogant insistence that he was not a negro had earned him nothing but mockery. Various get-rich-quick schemes and quixotic quests had filled his days and emptied his purse. He was amazed and grateful that he still had his health, a wonder considering the profession of his accustomed companions of the evening.

Unease bubbled within, a dissatisfaction with his empty past but more with the bleak future it promised. Clearly this once-in-a-lifetime e-clipse could mark a dramatic beginning to a new life, at least for him, if he could see a way clear to go on the lam, break free of the life he'd been leading. When walking away from your old friends it's necessary to break cleanly, to avoid the taps of drawn-out farewells or 'one-last-time's. His crew would look for him and he would be gone, only wild memories, odd mementoes and a nickel-colored underwater boat remaining. They'd be okay.

Maybe he wasn't the only one feeling like this? No, no, he was sure his crew all felt content with the occasional excitement, injuries, wealth and poverty of the life they'd chosen. Maybe Juan? But if Juan left the crew Nofina was sure the others would end up shot in the gut or swinging from a scaffold. No, Juan had to stay. If he wanted out he'd have to sort out his escape on his own.

He looked at the partially deflated balloon on the aft deck, shifting in the breeze like a great white jellyfish. "Juan, I'll take one more look from above. Let's launch the balloon again, I'll see what I can see."

"*Si*," he echoed, "but it is almost the day. If there is a better spot I hope it is not distant. And I hope it is near mooses."

"I saw them before, but they must have wandered off. I wonder what a moose call would sound like? Maybe, while I'm up above, you can try various moosey calls, and if I see them trotting towards you amorously I'll holler down. How's that?"

"'Amorously'?" Juan repeated nervously.

Nolana slapped his shoulder. "Come on, you've got water between you and the shore. What could they do?"

"They could swim. Mooses swim, this I know. And they do not like being fooled."

"Huh. Well, if one comes over, just go below, maybe submerge."

Juan looked uneasy but nodded slowly. "*Si, jefe*," he said, then went aft to ready the balloon for launch again.

"Look, Juan, I just want to take the balloon up to the end of the leash, get a proper eyeful of this Alaska I've heard about. Some say there's gold up here. Now, I know I won't see that from above, but who knows what I *will* see. Just like with the e-clipse, this is a once-in-a-lifetime experience. And we still have more H2 in the first bottle."

Once the balloon was inflated again with the cryptic 'H2' Nolana climbed into the basket below and nodded to Juan to release him. As he lurched upward he looked down at Juan and the Nautilus, his heart heavy. "Farewell, Juan, my old pal," he murmured, daring not to alert his old friend to his scheme.

Last night Nolana had loosened the clamps that bound the balloon's tether to its wheel. When the balloon reached its end the wire would pull free and Nolana in his basket would drift free, to the southwest if he judged the winds aright. He hoped his new life wouldn't end on the stony slopes of a mountain, to be devoured by a grizzly bear or pack of wolves, maybe even stomped by an amorous moose—but great rewards came from great risks.

FAYE WIPED HER DAMP sleeve across brow, exhausted but happy and content in a way she'd never before felt. She'd just handed a squalling girl to her mother, ragged and weary and full of joy as she looked at her child, then took her to her breast like a Madonna, her face radiant with tender love and peace. Faye's own heart swelled at the sight, and her faith she had helped bring that child into the world, into her mother's arms.

She had one more task, one more caring gift for the new mother. Mentally digging through her grandmother's lessons she remembered a few post-partum herbs. Scouring through her gladstone she found her hibiscus, lavender, rose hips and lemon balm, dropped them into the remains of the whiskey blend and shook the corked bottle.

Only then did she notice Emily standing by – had she been there the whole time? Grateful for the woman's surprising kindness and decency she looked up, quiet pleading in her exhausted eyes. "Emily, I hope you can help here. I don't know where the father is or Mary's destination. Can you watch over her, at least until one of you leaves this train? Give her a mouthful of this when she wakes up, but don't let her have it all too fast. Faye looked skeptically at the half-full bottle "This is meant to be enough for two – make it three days. I know you'll be getting off soon to detour to Denver, and I understand this isn't what you came out west for, but please do what you can to make sure she understands. Please?"

Faye realized that helping her, helping this new mother in a third-class car, was not the sort of thing that Vassar girls did. Already Emily courted ostracism, becoming a pariah in her group – an insular group isolated from its normal environment and very wary of the appeals to assimilate in this wild, impulsive land. The knives poised at Emily's back were not literal, but almost as lethal.

Faye's relief at Emily's swift response was almost immediate. "I'll do what I can. I think I heard her talking to another passenger, telling her that her husband – Brian – is in the army, posted at Fort Keogh. Mary was travelling to meet him when his discharge comes through, any day now." She turned pensive. "I wonder how they'll do, the three of them, out here."

Faye surprised herself when a mildly mischievous thought bubbled up from some unconventional bit of her brain. She blamed the levity on her own fatigue. "Suggest to the mother – Mary, was it? – suggest that she tell the babe it was born on the twenty-ninth, in the shadow of the eclipse." She considered a bit. "Or does that sound too ominous?"

Emily nodded.

"Ah, well, it was just an idea, add a bit more drama to the babe's birth – I wonder where she'll tell people she was born? Always an option for later, I suppose. It's not as if I'll be filling out a certificate – 'place of birth' would be difficult to pin down, don't you think? 'Somewhere in South Dakota or Wyoming'!" she laughed a little. "Who know, had it been more difficult she might have traversed the entire nation in the birth canal."

Emily laughed, shrugged. "You go rest yourself, now, Victoria. You've done some good work this day."

"Maybe the babe won't celebrate the eclipse, but I shall. I've taken a new name, you know. I declare that from this day forward I shall be known as Faye D'Accompli."

"So you're sticking to that. The girls heard and thought it was a lark – but I like it. Go rest now, Faye, frontier medicine woman."

Faye nodded, looked at the afterbirth but realized that, despite its uses she just couldn't take advantage of them then. When she struggled to stand, her back, her hips, her aching shoulders reminded her they'd been heartily abused for the past few hours. Once erect she shook off some stiffness and left the compartment, aware of the passengers' sly inspection of the redskin woman with her buckskin pants, bustier and gladstone who presumed to think she was a doctor – but she didn't care. Faye D'Accompli did not give a damn about them and their opinions, even less once she collapsed gracelessly in her own seat. Her body was exhausted but her mind stayed busy, thinking ahead, considering alternatives.

Why stop at a name? Victoria did not wear buckskins, and her bustier had long been buried where it would never meet a man's eyes. Her skin, her cheekbones and hair were unchangeable, integral parts of her self-image. No matter how long she studied in Poughkeepsie at Vassar, no matter what refined manners she mimicked, no matter what foreign tongues and thoughts she absorbed she was still proudly Wyandotte, still a woman of the Missouri plains, tied anciently to Lake Huron.

When the train steamed into Billings she debarked, checked the schedule by the ticket office and a map, grinned and sought out the druggist. A nearby hot spring was a short trip out, so Faye packed up her new purchases and her luggage and rode out from the livery stable in search of steamy relaxation.

WHO NAMED IT THE 'CLARK/Lurie' expedition, and by what logic were the names in that order? "Lurie and Clark" had a kind of familiarity to it, it fit easily into readers' minds and mouths. And he, Hank Lurie, *he* was the one arranging the transportation and recording the scenery and adventures – even creating them when necessary. And it was *he* who had selected their precise destination, based on his extensive reasearch in illustrated western adventure magazines and 'interviews' he conducted in bars with the more loquacious customers, whose tongues responded well to alcoholic lubrication.

Such were Hank Lurie's thoughts as the paddle steamer tied up just below the falls. "They seem to have neglected to include civilization around this dock," Mr. Clark looked around in vain for any kind of service. There wasn't yet a saloon or hotel, only a drygoods emporium in a canvas tent and a mule-drawn wagon waiting with a load of coal. He had an idea, a question for the skinner. "I say, whereabouts did you acquire that coal, my good man?"

The driver gestured with his chin. "Train station half-a-mile back."

That's encouraging, Clark thought. "Why didn't they put this dock there, then?"

At the driver's disdainful look he answered himself. "Quite right, quite right, of course you're not the fellow to ask."

Once the coal was offloaded for the steamer's return trip Lurie lugged their luggage to the wagon and asked the price to get to the train station, where he'd read that horses and mules were available for the last stage of their journey. When the driver told him the cost to take them and their bags in the coal-black cart a half-mile he laughed, incredulous. "Are you kidding?"

"Nope. You can walk if you like, go ahead and rent yourselves some animals, then come back and maybe find your bags haven't moved. Or maybe they have. Things like that happen around here."

"One of us could go ahead, and the other remain and stand guard," Lurie objected.

"Yep. Is it the English fella goin' ahead, or be he the one stayin' back?"

On principle Lurie objected to being taken advantage of, but the driver had a point. Lurie suspected that many times before the fellow had had discussions much like the one just shared with Lurie. He looked in the wagon's bed and opted against allowing his clothes to touch the black dust, but the trunk and bags were different. "All right, then, just take our gear and we'll walk."

"Don't matter none. Same price, either way."

"Of course."

Once they were underway Lurie sought to salvage some local color, a tale of enterprise from the driver. "Are you the only driver on this route?"

"Yep. It's a rough route. Other wagons been known to break their axles, mules get sick. Only me and my pair survive."

"Odd, that," offered Clark. "Almost like the Divine Hand is caring for you."

"Yep. Almost."

"Are there plans to extend the rail line to the dock, or smooth out this road?"

"Yep, they talk a lot but their words don't come to nothin'. See," he pivoted on his bench seat, "those folks as want the road fixed don't stick around long enough to pay for it, and those that stick around don't see cause to make the journey easier for them as are comin' anyway. Might be they prefer the new arrivals tired and wore out."

By shared looks both Lurie and Clark could see the other saw the logic of the situation, and the driver's pricing scheme.

At the station the wagon halted and the driver took in the two explorers. "Well, here we be. Get your gear off and I'll be on my way."

The pair looked distastefully at their begrimed bags and equipment trunk, looked around for a hardy soul to assist. "I say, are there no stevedores about?"

"Doesn't look that way." Lurie looked at the impatient driver. "You're leaving now, with or without our possessions, aren't you?"

"You have the right of it." He looked up at a steepled town clock.

"In London, or Southampton, even Liverpool they've motorized lorries to lift and transport any variety of loads. When I considered this adventure I did not anticipate all the conveniences I would be compelled to forego."

"Yes, well, that's life on the frontier." Lurie grunted as he slid the trunk down with a solid 'thunk' and cloud of black dust, then plopped the bags on the trunk or the ground, "Chock-full of surprises of all sorts. I hope you don't find it unbearable." As they watched the wagon creak away Clark asked, "Well, Mr. Lurie, what's next?"

Lurie spied a hotel across the muddy road. "Stay here, I'll get help."

In a quarter hour they were gratefully remarking on the shortcomings of their two-bed room, and looking forward to a proper bath. The twenty-ninth was still a few days away and they could afford a day of rest, and Lurie was glad of another opportunity to update accounts of their trip.

At the station Lurie sent off his long posts and paid, then watched the telegrapher's finger tap out his tales. "Say, you're that writer from back east, aintcha?" asked the clerk. "The one who's headin' out to see the e-clipse with that limey gent, right?"

"Well, yes, in fact I am."

"Huh. I've been readin' your words, and have to wonder—is that all true? I mean, what you wrote, did all that happen? Did *any* of it happen?"

What's the difference? Lurie asked himself for the thousandth time in his career. "Of course it's all true! You read it in the paper, didn't you? Right there in black and white?"

"Well, I s'pose so, but you don't look nothin' like the picture in the paper."

Picture? That was the first he'd heard of pictures. A part of him wanted to see what the world believed he looked like – but not just then. "Sometimes the draughtsmen take liberties."

The clerk squinted at him, then nodded. "I reckon they do."

Cryptic, thought Lurie, lingering in case the fellow asked for an autograph. Before the silence became embarrassing he left, determined to find a newspaper or two and learn what he looked like before returning to his companion in the hotel.

V

Glorious freedom overwhelmed Nofina Nolana as his wicker basket raced before the wind. He wanted to dance, to leap about, to sing or shout, but those didn't come as naturally or easily as laughter, especially in a wicker basket. Alone in the great swirling Alaskan blue he laughed in delight, laughed in unbounded joy at the impossible variety of options before him. Whenever, wherever he alighted he would revel in freedom.

His former companions and their narrow impressions of him, the living victims of his crimes, the nefarious circle of buying and selling and cheating that paid his way – all were only history, only dusty residue lingering in his black soul. And black he knew his soul to be – too often had he heard the words of the wise women, felt the pangs of abandoned opportunity, ruthlessly mocked the decent impulses that arose in his breast.

His laughter died, banked in his heart like glowing embers through the coming night's chill. The great question for him now was if he could move past the impulsive rogue he'd long been and somehow become worthy of trust. The buoyant balloon could not lift the heaviness of his guilt, the brilliant sun glowing on the snowy slopes could not wholly dispel the sable shadows in his psyche.

Like a cork on a flood his basket swept ahead through a pass, crags and cliffs speeding past him as he headed to ... his destiny, his fate, his new life.

It grew cold, terribly cold. He could endure cold with the best, he'd been on the sea through bone-chilling fogs and sleets, but here he had neither cabin nor foc'sle to retreat to, nothing beyond his peacoat and watch cap. He hunched down behind the wicker wall, peering over the top, helpless to bear right or left, trusting the winds to shape his path. How long would he be up here, and when he came to earth would it be among boulders, snow, trees or summer flowers? At least his flight was southwest, to the sunny plains as he'd hoped.

It was mid-morning before low mists thinned and he finally saw green below – this was the place! Boiling black clouds churned overhead, dragging skirts of rain across the plain below. Lightning flashed, thunder boomed, and the sluggish brain of the balloonist wondered what might happen to a balloon in a thunderstorm.

At last the wild swings and roaring winds and thunder convinced him that yes, definitely, it was time to come down. His icy fingers fumbled at the vent line, released the 'H2' from the envelope above. His basket dropped abruptly, his stomach following soon after. This would need a fine touch – no problem, everybody knew Nofina had a fine touch, as long as he didn't freeze first or be hit by lightning. As carefully and delicately as his bluing fingers could manage he coaxed the balloon lower, lower, lower, until scant dozens of feet separated his feet and the tree crowns blurring by below.

He'd just reached the flowery field and was opening the vent all the way when the lightning struck the nemol web above and raced down the trailing tether to earth. Nofina Nolana's new life began with an explosion above, a fireball, a massive shock and burn, and a mad drop on to columbine and Indian paintbrush.

THE WARM SPRING WAS deserted – how was it that people weren't thronging to this natural gift? Anyway, if she had it to herself that was okay with her. She stripped down and eased in, lightly scrubbed her underclothes, shirt and bustier before settling down on a smooth rock to relax. It felt so good, such a relief after – well, after everything – that she didn't want to stir, just to melt, but her plans demanded setting aside extra time for her hair.

Once she applied the soda/peroxide mix to her clean hair she would have an hour to scrub or lounge before rinsing with the lavender/chamomile/burdock root infusion she had already made up in her bag.

The hour, more or less, passed all too fast. The water hadn't cooled, the stone hadn't grown lumps, and her body argued for lingering and catching the next train. Rising even just to retrieve her lavender concoction took a major effort of will. Her eyes closed to protect them from the soda mix she knelt before her bag and rummaged for the jar when she felt a shadow fell across her.

Squinting up she saw only a ragged silhouette. "Hey, Indian girl, wanna smoke my peace pipe?"

Without thinking her fingers found her Bowie knife. "Among my people the women are most feared. You have heard of the Commanche, the Apache? Strong men kill themselves before they are captured, fearful they will fall into the hands of these women, experts in torture." Slowly she withdrew the blade. "It is said they can keep a man alive for three days while they slowly cut away pieces of him. Usually his voice wears out in the first day, so his screams cannot be heard, but I believe in my bag I have a remedy for that.

"Do you care to test it for me?" she stood, the concoction in her left hand, the knife in her right, goosebumps stippling her skin. She dropped her voice. "Too long it has been since I peeled the skin from a white man, castrated him, bound him in the sun in a wet skin on a scorpion's nest. I feel generous today – I shall permit you to choose how your death begins this day. And make no mistake – you will die -—but not today. Maybe tomorrow, maybe the next day. Choose." The warm west wind blew from the prairie, curled across her bare skin, drying it, but she felt none of it, heard nothing, saw only the man before her, awaiting his tell. What would he do?

Like a mesmerist's watch the gently swaying knife tip held all his attention. His hand dropped to his revolver. Faye smiled. "About now you might be wondering just how fast I am. And how fast are you? Well, the fact is, up to about twenty feet a woman with a knife will beat out a man with a holstered revolver. Or so the gamblers say. But maybe you want to test those odds. Ask yourself, do you feel lucky today?"

The stranger licked his lips, cleared his throat, backed up a step and put up his hands. "No harm meant, miss, just tryin' ta be friendly. No need for the knife, or for ... any of that. I'll just be movin' along then, if you don't mind?" He backed away two more steps, stumbled on a small stone and Faye imitated a war cry. He spun about, stumbled again and vamoosed like a terrified fool, but Faye couldn't find it in herself to laugh.

Soon Faye heard the hooves galloping away – and yet she stood, naked and still as the world and its sensations awakened in her again. The wind still sighed across the grasses, the sun had begun warming her, the sage scented the air, the waters called to her, warm and friendly. Finally, alert as a field mouse, she went back in the waters, not as gracefully as before, her knife and jar filling her hands. After a bit she let out a great gasping sob and soon after the shaking stopped. In time she felt safe enough to duck her head, scrub the bleach from her scalp and then massage in her herbal rinse.

Once dry she put her damp underclothes and linen shirt into her bag, refreshed her 'outfit,' and rode back to town. The hostler goggled at her, and when she looked in the mirror at the station she was shocked at the woman who looked back.

The Faye D'Accompli looking back was a blond with black brows and dark eyes. She believed that hers was a most beguiling look, and winked at reflection – but there was no hiding the fierceness in those black eyes either. She would take care in the testosterone-soaked frontier, and others would have to take care also. If she hurried she would still catch her train to Yellowstone Lake, and from there ...? Somehow find the ideal site to live precious minutes in the moon's shadow.

After that? In her life on the Wyandotte reservation she'd heard tales of young men going on spirit quests, where a boy would become a man and see his way before him. Was it vain and foolish of Faye to see this journey as her own spirit quest, and hope for revelations of her own future?

ALTOGETHER THE TOWN blooming around the rail station impressed Lurie pleasantly. It wasn't grand, the streets weren't paved, there was neither electricity, municipal water nor sewer, but he felt obliged to salute anything thriving way out in the west end of nowhere, the Wyoming territory. Lurie longed to interview some residents, learn what drew these hardy folks to leave their communities back east to build new lives in this place—*what were they finding, what were they escaping?* After all, the phenomenon bringing him and Clark would soon be history, but he cooled his curiosity about the frontier people. He was too aware of the passing of days until the eclipse to allow himself that journalistic detour. Maybe on the way back, unless he and Clark continued on to ...?

Lurie suspected that Mr. Clark *was* enjoying the liberty of exploring while Lurie assumed the burden of arrangements for pack animals, food, and camping supplies. He performed his duties competently, although with some resentment, and it wasn't until mid-afternoon that he felt he'd worked out the logistics to his satisfaction, so they might leave early the next morning.

He'd just heaved a sigh of relief for annoying tasks completed and was surveying the town again when he espied the striking copper-skinned blond in buckskin leaving the station and bearing her own bags. Suddenly his day brightened – there was no chance Clark would stumble across a jewel like this before he would! And she was unaccompanied, too!

"Good day, miss, it appears you've only just now arrived in town. Perhaps you have some questions, seek some guidance?"

Her wary eyes looked him over, saw no threat, turned her lips to her most southern belle demure smile. "Perhaps, kind sir. Would you be so kind as to bear my bags to the hotel yonder?"

"My pleasure." Yikes, the woman was an Amazon, her bags must weigh fifty pounds! "Do you intend to remain in town for long?" he grunted and gasped. At the step up he tottered for a moment, then by will alone conquered the second step.

Did she suppress a smile as she watched him struggle? "No, I'm heading toward the mountains to observe the eclipse."

"Are you indeed? By yourself?" he was honestly shocked. "My companion and I leave tomorrow early with the same goal, finding the ideal site to observe one of Nature's grandest displays, the celestial dance! Perhaps we might join together – these wild regions pose many risks," he said quietly at the front desk and dropped her bags. He looked at her, not quite pleading – acquiring a beauty for their trek would surely brighten their days, and perhaps his nights. And she was no dummy, she knew something of the eclipse, too! What a bonus for his readers, and for his journal of their adventure. "Pardon me, miss, allow me to introduce myself – Henry Lurie. My friends call me Hank, and I invite you to do so also."

The clerk arrived. "Faye D'Accompli, Hank" she said to Lurie, "and a room for the night, please," to the clerk. Back to Lurie. "Mr. Lurie – 'Hank'—" she interrupted herself, "I'm inclined to take you up on your offer. The eclipse is but three days hence. I trust you have a precise destination in mind?"

"I do, the most beautiful valley you'll ever see, with excellent visibility. Once you're settled in your room perhaps we can set you up with your pack animals, a tent of your own, and supplies. As it happens, my companion and I are staying here also, in room seven. I shall await your knock, Miss D'Accompli." He doffed his hat then turned to run up the stairs when he remembered there was no bellhop. With far less bounce he carried his new friend's bags up to her room – number five.

Once she was resting Lurie returned to the station to send more texts, urging his readers to welcome a woman to the expedition. Beyond that truth, every word he printed about Faye was a product of his imagination – and how his imagination did soar!

And so it was that two days later as the trio entered the valley under threatening skies they saw a white balloon racing toward them from the northwest. In wonder and puzzlement they stopped and watched, speculating what the rider might be up to, where he was headed, if they might meet him. All were surprised when Clark declared, "I say, it's descending, and quite rapidly at that!"

As if chasing the balloonist thunder boomed and a curtain of torrential rains began its sweep across the valley. "Yes, he's coming down, but he'll still get drenched!" agreed Faye.

"But why here? Is this a secret balloon-launching site?" cried Lurie over the roar of the rain and another explosion when a bolt obliterated a nearby tree.

"I daresay he's unwilling to test his balloon's safety in a lightning storm."

"Makes sense," muttered Lurie. "Could be he's not quite the fool I took him for," just as the balloon exploded in a ball of flame and plummeted to the earth.

VI

Lurie and Faye raced to the smoking remains of the balloon while Clark took the bridle of a mule in his right hand and followed as fast as the mule permitted. "Whatever shape the poor devil is in he'll find you a welcome sight," he assured the creature. "Except this might be in the way," he added as he freed the lever-action Henry and pointed it earthward on his left as they hurried to the catastrophe.

"He's not here!" yelled Lurie.

"He's not here!" echoed Faye.

Well, with that bolt the fellow surely got a jolt – where might he have flown to? Ah, there was a cedar with multiple broken limbs on one side. "Look over there!" he gestured with the carbine. Immediately the pair headed over.

Clark was still a few dozen yards away from them when Lurie called, "Here he is!" And Faye added, "He's alive!"

"Splendid, splendid," he said not quite loud enough for anybody except the mule to hear. The mule halted, so Clark halted. He looked at the mule, then into the woods ahead. Beyond his two companions – and their newcomer, who was even now lurching to his feet – he espied a massive brown shape charging through the rain.

There was no point in Clark's calling out, warning his friends of the grizzly and its great razor-claws and huge teeth, gruesome death in a package of massive power and deadly ferocity. Just then the newcomer also saw murder racing at him and rasped, "Run!" as he pushed Faye behind him. He then leapt and shouted, hoping at least to distract the beast from the woman whose tender eyes he'd awakened to.

Clark planted the Henry's stock in his shoulder, levered in a round and waited. Just before it reached his friends Lurie heard its approach and stood, froze, while Faye looked back, torn between fleeing and standing by her guest. The grizzly stood, its eight-foot fury towering over them, its roar reducing them to jelly.

That was the moment Clark had waited for, and with one shot he silenced the bear, dropped it in place. Goggle-eyed Lurie stared at his saviour while Faye's eyes remained locked on the cause of her near-death experience – right until she fainted. "You – you – you," Lurie pointed at the carcass while staring at Clark.

"Yes, I" Clark answered. "How is your patient?"

Lurie took some seconds to re-orient his focus from the bear scant yards away to the man again unconscious at his feet. "Huh? What? Oh, yes, hard to say, really, he's unconscious. Looks well enough, though." He shook his head. "Imagine, flying in on a balloon across the mountains, likely freezing, finally coming down and getting hit by lightning and shot like a cannon ball into a tree, falling to earth, and apparently surviving all that – only to become a grizzly entrée."

"Or did you mean 'grisly entrée'?" asked Clark.

Lurie chuckled. "Or perhaps 'gristly'."

Enough. "Perhaps not."

Lurie looked chastened, as Clark felt was proper. "And Faye? Is she coming around? Should I have brought two mules?"

Lurie squatted and Clark heard gentle slaps and soft words. "Yes, she's coming around. She's a tough one."

She was indeed. "Mr. Clark, thank God for your quick action! I am – we are – forever in your debt. Please, bring the mule and we shall bear our new neighbor to camp."

Clark hoped the fellow didn't have any breaks. If so, drooping the 'balloonatic' across the animal's back would surely rouse him from his sleep most unpleasantly. After handing the carbine to Hank – "Fine firearm, that. Good to see the Americans have mastered that art" –

as gently as he could he laid the aviator on the mule's back, his legs straddling and his arms embracing, his head to the left of the mule's neck. The four returned to camp, all kinds of thoughts and worries burbling in three of their brains.

Once Faye had prepared a palette Clark laid the man down, took the Henry from Hank and replaced it in its holster. While Faye attended to the victim Lurie set about writing his account of the encounter. "Clark, I had no idea you could shoot like that – and thank God you could! Just think, Clark, what a tale! Did you know we're famous? They're calling you a new Phileas Fogg, Clark! But Jules Verne never came up with a story like this – wait, wasn't there something about octopi? But that was a different book, and not on land, either, so, no, sir, it is not anywhere near as, as, *impressive* as downing a charging grizzly!"

Clark seemed amused. "My friend, did you assume I was just an English fop? No, I've hunted and shot throughout the Empire." He chuckled. "Imagine if I were but a fop. I expect our journeys would all be terminating in the gut of that bear. No, my friend, never mistake breeding for weakness."

"He's coming around," announced Faye.

HIS EYES OPENED TO a beautiful blond woman's face. He considered feigning bewilderment, asking if she was an angel and he was in heaven – but he didn't want to begin his new life playing the flirt, the fop, the fool. No, he was a new man now, living a new life – but he couldn't help but grin at his good fortune. "How am I?"

She smiled back. "From out here you look well enough. How are things on the inside?"

He took a quick inventory then tentatively sat up. "Not bad, not bad at all!"

"Take it easy. You've been through a lot," she counseled.

"Yeah, just from what we've seen you rode a balloon across the Rocky Mountains, got hit by lightning and tossed at a cedar, then attacked by a grizzly bear. Yeah, I'd say that's a lot. And we don't even know what came before. Is your life always so exciting, friend?" asked a man's voice.

He didn't look at the man, imagined no reason to look away from his nurse. "Pardon me, miss, but I do believe an introduction is appropriate. My name is –" he struggled to tell the truth – "Jean Pierre Delacroix of New Orleans, although lately of … more remote lands."

"*Bonjour Monsieur Delacroix, je m'appelle Mademoiselle Faye D'Accompli.*"

"*Fait accompli,*" he smiled at her soubriquet. Cautiously he rolled into a squat then stood, checked his balance and offered Faye a hand up, then noticed two men studying him. One reached out, "*Je m'appelle Monsieur Jonathan Clark.* Pleasure to make your acquaintance, sir."

"Folks call me Hank Lurie. I'm a reporter, been spreading the word to the world about Mr. Clark's adventures coming west to see the eclipse."

"The e-clipse! Am I too late? Is it yet happened?" Jean-Pierre looked desperately from face to face, lingering on Faye's.

Hank answered, chanced a quick look at the now-clear deep blue above. "No need to panic, friend, it's not until tomorrow. And it looks like my promised clear skies will run true."

"The clouds, the thunder, lightning, rain … it's all over with and gone already?" wondered Delacroix.

"I hear tell the weather up here is many things, but never boring," explained Lurie.

The Englishman spoke. "Well, my friends, what do you say we have some bear meat for dinner today – and perhaps for the coming week. It is, if I say so myself, quite a large bear that I killed."

"Yeah, how'd you do that, Clark? One shot?"

The marksman shrugged. "I've hunted big game throughout the Empire. When he roared I shot through his mouth to his brain stem. If

I were so inclined I would try to save the pelt, but that's not why I came here, and it would prove a serious burden in further travels."

"Huh. About those further travels, mind if I come along while you carve up your kill, and we have a talk?"

"Not at all, I have a few suggestions. Allow me to retrieve my tools and we'll set to our labors."

TO NOBODY'S SURPRISE the handsome Creole gentleman and the beautiful Indian maiden spent the afternoon and next morning harvesting varieties of herbs and flowers Faye used in her healing. As they worked, and she taught him about the virtues and dangers in nature's medicines, they also laid out their lives as they never had before, never felt the freedom that arises from meeting another understanding soul before.

"*Ma belle* – do you sometimes wonder what would have happened, what you might have done, if you had met a certain other person at an earlier time? When you were yourself a different person? What I mean to say is – in my life I have been a terrible man, done terrible things, and although my gratitude knows no bounds for having met you now, there linger some regrets that we did not meet sooner. So many ... sins .. you might have kept me from. Perhaps your honest strength and virtue might have deflected me from the course that has tainted my soul forever."

In her squat she assumed a reflective pose, resting her elbow on one knee and her hand cradling her chin. "Would you have wanted to meet me as a girl on the Missouri reservation, ignorant of the ways of the world? Of what use would she be in taming you? Or the timid young woman entering the women's college in New York, trying to learn to pass as a woman of culture? Even now, during this impulsive journey that brought me here, only now am I awakened to my own wisdom and strength. No, *m'sieur*, if Fate meant us to meet that rendezvous could not happen before we were ready, until *I* became Faye and *you* remembered you are Jean Pierre." Even as she spoke the words Faye felt their truth resonating in her breast, felt the rightness of them.

He laughed. "All it took was for Fate to set the date for the moon to block out the sun's light! And for us to chase after that shadow, so ephemeral and fleeting." He shook his head. "You are right, I suppose. Had I met a woman like you in New Orleans I – I'll just admit I would not have recognized you, would not have appreciated you, the astronomer, the doctor, your strength, wisdom and kindness." He stopped, tilted his head. "To be honest, I believe that if I could have, I would have used you and then tossed you aside when done." Another pause. "Is it wrong that I sometimes miss those days, the life the war took from me, that destroyed my Creole society? I confess we, my family, had slaves."

"Do you want it back? Any of it?" The Wyandotte woman recalled her own people's ownership of others in her youth.

He looked down, felt himself falling into her eyes. "No, no, not really. It's just, well you may not know this yet but you will later, it's just that the days of our youth leave behind their savor of sweet wines, fine dances, glorious feasts, the ... the liberties permitted and taken. No matter how distant the memories they remain as vibrant, as full of life as they were the next morning. Vibrant and full of life is what we treasure most, *c'est vrai?*"

"I would not know. In this I shall trust the judgment of a man of far more years and experiences than I have," she teased.

"You see too clearly the man before you," he answered with a rueful shake of his head. "But not, I pray, too many more years to suit you."

"What's that?" asked Faye with an alert jerk of her head. Lord, please, not another bear! Or even a moose!

Jean Pierre harkened to the sounds, heard two voices, a man and a woman's, far off. Far off the new arrivals may be then but their campsite was their only possible destination. At least they were not practicing stealth. With an index finger urging quiet Jean Pierre slipped off in that direction, into the woods.

Clark and Lurie were hunched over the bear's remains, hanging great hunks of flesh over a smoky fire that popped and crackled. Faye sauntered turned her attention back to the animal track and soon saw a couple with pack animals, the man in an army uniform and the woman on a mule with a child at her breast.

The improbability of the situation proved to Faye its reality. "Mary?" What next to say to a woman you didn't know but whose child you had delivered? "You're well? And your daughter also?"

"Yes, well, when Brian arrived from the fort we were without plans and so I had a thought, said to meself, 'go where the Indian woman went, she'll know her way around, what to do, where to go, how to live'. So I asked about which way the Indian woman went and, well, here we are!"

"Mary just can't sing your praises loudly enough, miss," added her husband. "The army taught me a lot about army life, but not about makin' me way in the wilds of Montana, or Wyoming for that. We hope we're not imposing."

Faye felt embarrassed by their praise, by their faith – Missouri was not Wyoming was not Poughkeepsie. Yet, here she was, all eyes on her and full of trust. She looked around at the great basin with its animals, herbs, water and fresh air. She couldn't complain of being crowded. "Not imposing at all. In fact, I'm grateful you're here, so we can share the eclipse. It's due to begin soon."

The newcomers shared looks. "What is this eclipse?"

How to explain? "A shadow will fall across the face of the sun and darkness will blanket the land."

"Sounds biblical," worried Brian.

"But the blanket will be pulled away, the light will return, and soon the animals and plants will have forgotten. We, however, will remember this the rest of our days."

"Sounds biblical indeed," agreed Mary. "Oh, let me introduce our daughter to the woman who brought her into the world!"

"Welcome ... what is her name?"

"We haven't decided yet. Maybe you can help?"

"Perhaps name her in commemoration of this day of celestial magic. 'Artemis Phoebe' perhaps, after the sun and moon?" suggested Jean Pierre as he emerged from the forest.

"Ah, Jean Pierre, allow me to introduce Mary and Brian and their daughter – 'Artemis Phoebe'?"

"I can't say I understand all this, but I like the name, it gives our girl some elegance, some class," her father said.

SCIENTIFICALLY THE eclipse was exactly as Faye expected it to be, each stage just as described in her readings. The ever-larger bites of the disc, the gradual darkening of the land, the quieting of the animals, the hush settling on the world – all was precisely as laid out in her imagination all those months ago back in Poughkeepsie.

What she had not anticipated and still did not understand was the effect of the celestial miracle on her own soul, the impossible promise of a 'once-in-a-lifetime' event living up to the advertising. She was torn, she wanted to look around, see how the mid-day darkness leached color from the world, to harken to the sudden silence disturbed only by the ignorant happy babbling of their creek, to savor the suddenly shifting breezes responding to the swift fluctuations in temperatures – but she could not bear to take her eyes away from the awesome splendor of the heavenly spectacle.

"Dear Lord," Jean Pierre murmured at her side. Could he possibly be feeling all she felt, wondering at these mad thoughts? "Yes," summed it all up as best she could.

At the edge of her awareness she heard Clark sliding photographic plates into and out of his camera and Lurie diligently packing them away, noticed the gasps and prayers of Brian and Mary, the gibberish of the child – and all that would be sorted out later, when she refined her impressions, put words to the mysteries and the mundane.

Unconsciously her hand sought out Jean Pierre's and found it was seeking hers. These once-in-a-lifetime magical moments, this experience shared by two souls experiencing freedom in ways they never before had, whispered to Faye of the wonders of the Plan for the world and all its creatures, reminded her that an abundance of miracles, great and small, teased at her from every fallen leaf and towering cedar. She bathed in the glory and squeezed Jean Pierre's hand in speechless, awe-struck wonder at the marvel of the heavens.

She breathed, she supposed she must have, but her abrupt gulp of air when the first fingernail of the sun edged out of the shadow brought her back to the normal world – which would never again be 'normal' for her. She and Jean Pierre shared a look, long and amazed and grateful for these moments together with the other, who was no longer an 'other'.

As the world brightened Faye felt such a sense of loss and gratitude and promise. She knew such seconds were unique gifts, felt forcing the wonder beyond its natural boundaries would not make her days special so much as diminish the unique magic of what she and Jean Pierre – for she was sure he felt much as she did – had just shared. Yet also she knew this magic would surprise in unexpected ways, would shape and color her remaining days.

Before the splendor was done with and routine life returned to the camp Faye whispered the only word she could think might explain her feelings. "Hallelujah," she sighed, then looked at Jean Pierre who removed his smoked-glass goggles and wiped his eyes. "*Mon Dieu*," he echoed.

CAMP THAT NIGHT WAS quiet, restful, despite everybody's plans for the morrow. Before Faye went to her tent she faced Jean Pierre, took his hands in hers and a carefree grin bubbled to her mouth and Jean Pierre nodded, then the pair laughed in agreement. After a tender kiss they parted, their hearts joyful. It was good to be alive!

While packing up the next morning the shadow-chasers spoke in hushed tones of what they had seen and felt. Lurie and Clark would continue their cross-continental journey, bear south to Denver and then ...?

Jean Pierre considered recommending some San Francisco establishments if they were heading that way, but decided against it, as that part of his life was done with. And for him? What plans did he have? "Faye D'accompli, will you marry me?" he surprised her, and himself to be honest. "Yes, yes!" she surprised herself. "But we don't have a preacher!" "Nor a priest," he added.

Lurie heard the commotion and guessed at its cause. "Faye, Jean Pierre, it's not quite the same thing, but I believe Mr. Clark would be amenable to make some sort of benediction with his high-class speech. It's not a church ceremony, but I reckon people out here will have to make-do for a while, and I suppose that marrying and baptizing are good starts."

"Baptizing? It's early for that, isn't it?" laughed Faye.

Lurie nodded to Mary, Brian and tiny Artemis Phoebe at the creek with Mr. Clark. "Life goes on," the bride whispered.

When the camp was packed up farewells were taken and Mr. and Mrs. Delacroix returned to the burgeoning town to open a proper apothecary bankrolled by Jean Pierre's hidden double eagles, while Brian and Mary and Artemis saw fit to build a cabin, a homestead and a life in the cozy valley. Once a month or so they promised to trek to town for supplies and to share memories and dreams with the only people who had chased shadows with them on that July afternoon of eighteen-seventy-eight.

As they rode off Faye took a last look back at the valley, thanking the provider for the openhanded blessings showered upon her, upon all of them. A clean, cool wind mussed her glossy raven hair, Jean Pierre grinned, his hand sought hers, and she grinned back and looked ahead.

EPILOGUE

A quarter-century later a Swiss patent clerk who contemplated Big Questions was poring over prints made from the Clark-Lurie plates, and a flaw caught his eye. It looked like a distant star had somehow ducked in front of the sun's darkened disc.

If this wasn't a flaw, then what could explain it? Could it be that the sun's gravity warped empty space, bent the light waves, and made the star shift to appear where it wasn't? Newton, Copernicus, Kepler could not account for this image. What, Alfred Eisenstein wondered, could?

The End

"History is Bunk"
attributed to Henry Ford

Dear Readers, I admit to extensive liberties in this novelette. As far as I know <u>none</u> of the characters I incorporated in this work ever existed, or said or thought <u>any</u> of the things I attribute to them anywhere.

Similarly the geography is not to be trusted. Rather, dear readers, accept this as a steampunk fantasy romance.

I hope you see fit to post a glowing review of this work – I find occasionally I yearn for a message back from these bottles flung into the seas, and encouragement is welcome.

Also, you might find touring my website interesting – I know I do!

You may find it at Calliopesgears.com, which I share with Lindsay Peet, or for more privacy you may email me at lpetersen@calliopesgears.com.

Finally, dear reader, if I've roused a laugh or raised your pulse with my efforts, please take a few moments to post a glowing review on the site from which you purchased this book, or any and everywhere else people like you look for quality reads.

Lindsay Petersen

Don't miss out!

Visit the website below and you can sign up to receive emails whenever Lindsay Petersen publishes a new book. There's no charge and no obligation.

https://books2read.com/r/B-A-MXYNB-JORXE

BOOKS 2 READ

Connecting independent readers to independent writers.

Also by Lindsay Petersen

The Reluctant Chrononaut
Pleasures & Perils

The Romantic Chrononaut
Caught in the Wizards' Duel
Avatars of the New Age

Standalone
Shadow Chasers

Watch for more at https://www.calliopesgears.com/.

About the Author

Lindsay Petersen is a native of Leeds, Alabama, where she grew up feeling she had been born a century too late – and likely even in the wrong Leeds.

She's lived all over the world, but most enjoyed Paris, where she studied the French allure of l'amour, and Delhi where she won a coveted first in her studies of the Kama Sutra, excelling especially in her lab work.

She lives and travels with her husband, who calls himself "the luckiest man in the world." Lindsay Petersen agrees with him.

Read more at calliopesgears.com.